Little Ree

Written by **Ree Drummond**

Illustrated by **Jacqueline Rogers**

HARPER

An Imprint of HarperCollinsPublishers

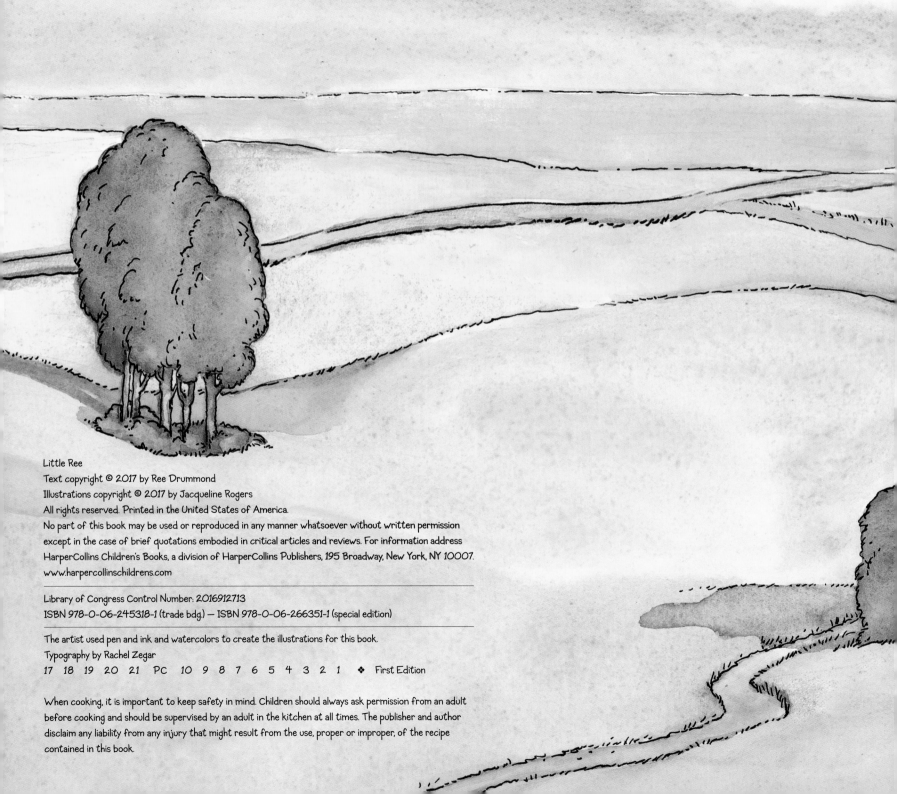

Library of Congress Control Number: 2016912713

ISBN 978-0-06-245318-1 (trade bdg.) — ISBN 978-0-06-266351-1 (special edition)

The artist used pen and ink and watercolors to create the illustrations for this book.

Typography by Rachel Zegar

17 18 19 20 21 PC 10 9 8 7 6 5 4 3 2 1 ❖ First Edition

When cooking, it is important to keep safety in mind. Children should always ask permission from an adult before cooking and should be supervised by an adult in the kitchen at all times. The publisher and author disclaim any liability from any injury that might result from the use, proper or improper, of the recipe contained in this book.

For accidental country girls everywhere
—Ree

For Tommy
—Jackie

Hi, I'm Ree.

A long, long time ago, I used to live in the city.

Well, it wasn't exactly a long long time ago.

It was yesterday, in fact.

Okay, okay, okay. Until exactly four hours and nineteen minutes ago,
if you want to be exact, I used to live in the city.

But I don't live there anymore!

Today, I moved to an old red house on my grandma and grandpa's ranch.

They need a little extra help these days.
And I'm just the girl for the job!

It was hard to leave home, but Grandma
says I'm going to love being a country girl!

I brought my mom, my dad, and my little brother with me, of course.

And my dog, Puggy. And my favorite cat, Patches.

And just a couple of other things, too!

I'm sure going to miss my friends. And the ice cream store.
And ballet class and the park down the street and the pool.

Hey! I guess you could say that I LIVE
in a park now! And look—my very own pool!
Ahhhh . . . just smell that fresh, clean air.
I feel like a country girl already!

Ew . . . Mikey?
What . . . is THAT?!?

YUCK!

Maybe I don't want to know. That's a
little too much country for me.

Grandma is so excited I'm finally here! She says she doesn't know how she's gotten by this long without me.

Oh, I love Grandma so so so so so so so soooooooooooo much. To the moon and back, and to the stars and back, and to the sun and back. I love Grandma to infinity.

And guess what? She even made a country girl bedroom just for me.

Hmmm. This is different from my old bed. My old bed was big
and fluffy and white and fancy.

This bed is brown. And . . . BROWN! And not very fluffy at all.

But don't worry. I have a fix for that!

That's more like it! Now it feels a little more like home.

It's already time for bed. Grandma says I need some shuteye because she is waking me up at the crack of dawn. I don't know what "crack of dawn" means, but I DO know that tomorrow will be my first real morning on a real ranch as a real country girl.

Grandma's right. I really should get some shuteye.

WHAT in the world is THAT?
The country sure is noisy! How's a girl supposed
to get any shuteye around here?

Is this . . . is this the crack of dawn? But I feel like I just went to bed.

It's dark outside.

My eyes won't open.

How come my legs won't move?

Okay, okay. I'm awake now!
And it sure is a good thing. Grandpa
and I have LOTS of work to do.

Grandpa just saddled my new horse for me.
He says Pepper can be all mine!

Puggy, Patches, and Pepper.
Perfect!

Grandpa has to help me onto the saddle. By tomorrow, he probably won't need to help me at all. I should be a pro by then!

Okay, Pepper: Let's GO!

Pepper?

chomp
chomp
chomp

Hey, it worked!
Pepper is going in the right
direction . . . and so are the cattle!

Pepper!?!?!
You're eating AGAIN!?!?

Wrong way, Pepper! Wrong way!

Argh!
How come I got
the one horse that
doesn't behave?

Finally. That was the longest morning of my whole entire life. Maybe I'm not cut out for this country girl thing after all. I don't think the cows even like me.

And I know Pepper doesn't like me.

Thank goodness . . . it's breakfast time! Or is it
lunchtime? Or is it brunchtime?
    I have no idea what time it is!

All I know is, I am HUNGRY! I feel like I haven't eaten in years!

Grandma and I are going to make pancakes. At least THAT'S something I'm good at.

Grandma says I make the best pancakes ever!

The meal is served, ladies and gentlemen!

Pepper! You've already had breakfast. TWICE!

If I didn't know any better, I'd think that horse was out to get me.

Yawwwn. I feel a little sleepy all of a sudden.
This country girl stuff is sure . . . hard . . . work. . . .

Oh no! I overslept! And all the cousins are coming over for a barbecue today! I can't wait to meet them. I hope they like me!

I'd better go get ready. I have to look just right.

Now, which shoes, which shoes . . . I have to find the perfect shoes. . . .

Yes! These are definitely the ones.
I'm all ready to meet my cousins!

Oh no. I'm wearing the wrong clothes.
AND the wrong shoes.
I don't think I'll ever be a country girl.

Or maybe I will! My cousins are the best!

Ha ha! I knew my shoes would work out just right.
And look—even Pepper likes them.

I think this country girl thing just might work out after all.

Little Ree and Grandma's Pancakes

Makes 2 servings

Be safe! Always cook with an adult. Don't touch sharp knives or hot stoves and ovens!
And always wash your hands before and after cooking.

Ingredients

1 cup sour cream

7 tablespoons all-purpose flour

2 tablespoons sugar

1 teaspoon baking soda

1/2 teaspoon salt

2 whole large eggs

1/2 teaspoon vanilla extract

Butter, for frying and serving

Warm syrup, for serving

Instructions

1. In a small bowl, whisk together eggs and vanilla. Set aside.

2. In a separate small bowl, stir together flour, sugar, baking soda, and salt.

3. In a medium bowl, stir together the sour cream with the dry ingredients until just barely combined (don't overmix).

4. Whisk in the egg mixture until just combined.

5. Heat a griddle over medium-low heat and melt some butter in the pan. Drop batter by 1/4 cup serving onto the griddle. Cook on the first side until bubbles start to form on the surface and edges are starting to brown. Flip to the other side and cook for another minute. (Pancakes will be a little on the soft side.)

6. Serve with softened butter and syrup.